The Secret of the Seal

The Secret of the Seal

DEBORAH DAVIS

Illustrations by Judy Labrasca

Crown Publishers, Inc.
New York

Published by Crown Publishers, Inc.
225 Park Avenue South,
New York, New York 10003

CROWN is a trademark of Crown Publishers, Inc.

Printed in the U.S.A.

Library of Congress Cataloging-in-Publication Data
Davis, Deborah. The secret of the seal/by Deborah Davis.
SUMMARY: Ten-year-old Kyo, an Eskimo boy, faces a difficult
moral choice between friendship for a seal and loyalty to his
family. 1. Eskimos—Juvenile fiction. 2. Indians of North
America—Juvenile fiction. [1. Eskimos—Fiction. 2. Indians of
North America—Fiction. 3. Seals (Animals)—Fiction.] I. Title.
PZ7.D28586Se 1989 [Fic]—dc 19 88-39533

ISBN 0-517-56725-3

10 9 8 7 6 5 4 3 2 1

First Edition

The Secret
of the Seal

Pronunciation Key

Kyo	kē'·ō
Annawee	ă'·nă·wē
Kudlah	kōͦod'·lă
Ahko	ă'·kō

The settlement houses were small specks on the cove behind him when Kyo saw the hole in the ice. The blue-gray circle a short distance ahead broke into the white glare of the great frozen bay.

Although he was eager to see the hole close up, he moved cautiously. Every few steps he tested the strength of the snow-covered ice with his harpoon.

The opening was almost as wide as Kyo was tall, and he was surprised to find one so large. Inside its thick, ragged edges a brisk wind rippled the water's surface.

1

Kyo found a small slab of ice nearby, carried it away from the hole, and lay down on his belly.

Hiding behind the slab, Kyo peered around it at the open water. Now and then passing clouds blocked the spring sun, and snowflakes whirled around him.

He waited and waited in his uncomfortable position. Nothing appeared. He was getting tired, and the excitement faded as his feet got cold. Soon his head dropped onto his arm, the ice blind fell over, and he dozed.

Thwack thwack! Kyo dreamed that his mother slapped fresh dough with her broad hands. *Thwack thwack!* His mouth watered from the smell of bread baking in the coal stove. *Thwack SMACK!* He opened his eyes.

Beside the hole, watching him, was a seal.

She rolled on her side and clapped her flappy feet—*thwack smack!* Kyo's pounding heart sounded louder to him than the seal's clapping flippers. Clutching his harpoon, he crept toward her slowly.

2

The seal gazed at him. Her flippers waved slightly. He rose to his knees and aimed the harpoon.

She rolled onto her back. The sun came out and made her belly shine like a silver hilltop.

Baffled by her fearlessness, Kyo heaved the sharp weapon into a mound of snow.

He sat back on his heels, rested his chin in his hands, and frowned.

"What is your name?" Kyo asked the seal. She rolled onto her stomach and moved closer to the hole. "Is it Tooky?" Kyo asked, using the first name that came to him.

The seal plunged headfirst into the water. Kyo peered down after her but couldn't see the animal swimming under the icy waves.

"How does a seal stay under water so long?" Kyo asked his mother, Annawee, that night.

Annawee, Kyo, and his father, Kudlah, were eating dinner in the room that was kitchen, living room, and Kyo's bedroom. Kyo put down his fork and took a deep breath.

"Do you want more stew?" his mother asked.

Kyo looked at her with his puffed cheeks and shook his head. His father laughed.

"Kyo, your face is turning red!" Kyo let out a *whoosh* and kept eating. He looked sad.

4

"What's wrong, Kyo?" asked Annawee.

"I could never be a seal," he said. His parents laughed.

"No, Kyo. You're a boy and you're going to be a man. Soon you'll kill a seal, not become one."

"Do you know how a seal stays under the water so long?" Kyo asked his father.

"I don't know," Kudlah replied, "but you don't need to know that to get one. You need patience to wait for a seal to surface and skill to greet her with your harpoon."

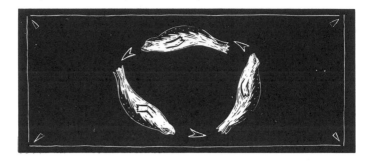

The next day Kyo returned to the hole in the ice. He didn't wait long. Tooky's whiskers burst out of the water, and her sleek body slithered onto the ice. Kyo inched toward her on his hands and knees.

She leaned away from him but did not swim off. When he was only an arm's length away, Kyo stopped.

"I want to be your friend," he said quietly. "I won't hurt you."

The seal stretched her head toward his and sniffed the air. Kyo froze and held his breath. Tooky came so close that her whiskers tickled Kyo's nose and he sneezed.

Tooky jumped backward.

"Wait!" Kyo cried, but the startled seal was already back in the sea.

Kyo knelt beside the hole. Moments later, Tooky's head popped up.

"I'm sorry I scared you, Tooky," apologized Kyo.

Tooky sniffed at his face and nuzzled him with her cold, wet nose. Kyo giggled and wiped his cheek with his sleeve.

"I wish I could visit the sea with you," Kyo said. "I've never gone anywhere."

Tooky slipped under the water. This time she didn't come back. Kyo shut his eyes and imagined undersea caves and somersaulting seals. They welcomed him to their home and chased each other around seaweed and rocks.

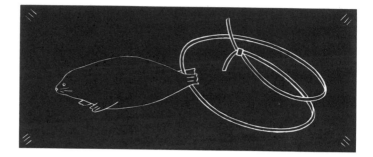

Kyo got restless waiting for Tooky the next day. He fished in his pockets and found a smooth gray stone.

The stone was tapered at one end and almost round in the middle, while the other end was flattened and flared, reminding Kyo of a seal's tail. He dug his knife out of another pocket and held it tightly.

Closing his eyes, he pictured a seal: rounded head, widely spaced eyes, blubbery neck, thick, full body, sleek tail.

Then he opened his eyes, half expecting to see the rock changed into the form of a seal. It was still just a rock. But now he could see the seal in it clearly and he began to carve.

Tooky's shining wet head poked up through the hole in the ice. She came out of the water and lay drying in the sun.

Kyo continued to carve, glancing frequently from the stone to the seal and back to the stone. Tooky rolled on her side just as Kyo finished the stone seal's head.

"Are you tired of holding still for me?" Kyo asked as he slipped the carving and knife back in his pocket.

Kyo put his hand lightly on Tooky's back and let his arm rest across her body. The seal rolled gently side to side, then with a quick shake threw his arm off.

Kyo draped one leg across her. Again she tossed him aside. Giggling, Kyo threw both an arm and a leg over her solid body. When she tossed him this time, he rolled away, laughing, then climbed on her back. He clung to her neck while she rocked back and forth, and he laughed so hard that he fell off.

Tooky prodded him with her nose and plopped down beside him. When Kyo lay his arm gently across her this time, she did not shake it off. She lowered her head, closed her eyes, and slept.

Clouds covered the sun, and a cool wind gusted over them. A little chilled, Kyo hid from the wind behind the seal and huddled close to her broad furry belly.

Her heart was a muffled *ba-boom, ba-boom* in his ear. He watched the little white puffs that formed and dissolved near Tooky's nose each time she breathed.

Suddenly, she stopped breathing. Kyo kept watching for the little breath-clouds, but when minutes had passed and none appeared, he sat up, alarmed.

Was she sick? he wondered. Was she dying?

His eyes blurred. He wiped them with a mitten. Crouching over her, he listened close to the seal's nose. He heard nothing.

Holding back tears, he pressed his ear to her body. *Ba-boom, ba-boom, ba-boom . . .* just like normal.

Tooky was awake now, watching him calmly. She didn't look sick, Kyo observed, and the little clouds were forming again every few seconds in front of her nose.

Kyo put aside his worried thoughts. For a while he and Tooky played together, and when the seal napped later on, he wasn't so surprised to see her breathing halt again.

This time he watched more patiently. He saw that she breathed between long pauses. He tried to hold his breath as long as she did, but it was impossible.

"Wake up, Tooky!" he called out when he had tired of his breath-holding game.

Tooky's eyes snapped open, and as Kyo had expected, her breath came faster. She wriggled toward the water and slipped away. Puzzling about her strange, slow breathing, Kyo headed for home.

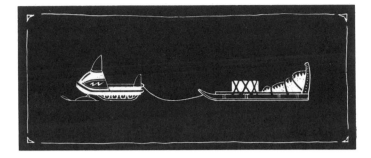

Why does Tooky's breathing slow down when she sleeps? Kyo was still wondering the next day as he helped his father untangle their sled dogs' traces. He was thinking of asking his father about the seal when the sound of a distant, unfamiliar hum distracted him.

The hum grew into a deep buzz, and then into a loud, growling whine. Kyo saw a man approaching on a snowmobile pulling a sledge. Kyo had seen snowmobiles, but no one in their small settlement owned one yet. He watched with wide eyes and an open

12

mouth as his uncle George drove the noisy contraption to his house and stopped.

Kyo had never met George, who lived far to the south in a big city. He didn't know much about him, except that his mother called him by his boyhood name, Ahko.

George was a tall man with a heavy mustache and the biggest black boots Kyo had ever seen. George told lots of jokes, and when he laughed Kyo felt the tiny house shake. Kyo liked it when Uncle George picked him up and swung him around by his hands. He liked it even more when he rode on top of his tall uncle's shoulders.

That evening during supper, George told Kyo, Annawee, and Kudlah about the big city zoo. They had never been to a zoo. George described how the animals lived in large cages and how the zookeepers brought them their food and water once a day. He drew pictures of lions, giraffes, gazelles, zebras, monkeys, and other animals that lived there.

"Do any seals live in the zoo?" asked Kyo.

13

"No," answered George, and Kyo smiled. He didn't think Tooky would like to live in a cage. But George had more to say about seals and zoos.

"No seals live there yet, Kyo. But I hope to change that."

"What do you mean, Brother?" asked Annawee.

"The zoo has built a special cage with a water tank," explained George. "They are offering a lot of money to someone who can sell them a healthy seal to live in it. So this is a very special trip for me. I get to see my sister and her family, and I will earn a good sum of money by bringing back to the city a plump, lively seal."

"I hope that you have come to the right place, Brother," said Annawee. "We are happy to see you after such a long time, but the seals have not been so plentiful this spring." Kudlah nodded his head in agreement.

Annawee ladled second helpings of steaming, savory stew into the men's bowls.

When she came to Kyo's place, he put his hand over his bowl.

"No, thank you," he said. "I am not hungry anymore."

In the morning Kyo ran all the way to Tooky's hole. When the seal appeared, Kyo flung his arms around her neck, not waiting until the dry air had absorbed some of the moisture from her thick fur.

"Oh, Tooky," he exclaimed breathlessly, "you must be very careful! My uncle is looking for a seal just like you!"

Tooky poked him with her nose.

"Not today, Tooky. We can't play out in the open today, and there's no place for us to hide together. You'll just have to go back into the ocean and stay away from here until my uncle returns to the city. And warn your friends. I don't think you'd like to be captured and put in a cage."

The seal prodded him again.

"I know you want to play," Kyo said firmly. "But it's too dangerous. My uncle might see us. Please go back into the water and hide." He stepped away from the seal. She waddled after him.

"No!" he cried. He pushed her gently toward the hole. "Go!" The seal gave him one long look, then slipped beneath the ice. Kyo walked back to his house, kicking at blurry clumps of ice and snow.

Geörge unloaded lumber and wire from the sledge behind the snowmobile. He began to build a large cage.

"Come help me, Kyo!" George called to the boy, who watched him uneasily.

Kyo hesitated. He liked this rare visitor and wanted to know him better, but didn't want to help him capture any seals.

"Kyo, I need an extra pair of hands to hold this wood in place while I nail it."

Kyo joined his uncle.

"Where did you go this morning?" George asked.

"For a walk," Kyo replied.

"It's pretty quiet around here," George went on. "What's there for a boy to do?"

"Lots of things," Kyo answered eagerly. "In the summer I like to fish. When I catch one, I kill it and clean it and give it to my mother to cook for dinner. Sometimes my father takes me hunting. When the weather's bad, I go to my collection of stones, pick one, and carve it." He pulled the leather thong that hung around his neck out of his jacket. Attached was a smooth white stone shaped like a seal.

"I have another one that looks like a bear." Kyo ran into the house to get the other carving. He brought it to his uncle, who looked at it closely.

"This is just like a bear, Kyo. You must watch the animals often to know exactly how they are shaped." He handed the bear back to Kyo.

"I do watch the animals," Kyo said. "I like to hunt with my father and play with my friends, but sometimes I like to go out by myself, not far from here. I sit very quietly for a long time and wait for the animals to come. I know where to find caribou trails and rabbit holes. I even know where there's a wolf den, and last spring I saw her pups!"

George listened as he bent wire around the wood frame.

"You must know where to find seals, too," said George.

Kyo was silent.

"Don't you watch the seals?" asked George.

"The seals are very special." Kyo spoke in a quiet voice.

"They are," George agreed.

"I don't think they will like living in a cage."

George stopped working and looked at the boy.

"I never really thought about whether they'd like it or not. I don't suppose they really care one way or the other. As long as they get fed—and the zookeepers give the animals as much as they want."

Kudlah joined them, shaking his head.

"It seems kind of strange," he told his

THE SECRET OF THE SEAL

brother-in-law. "Around here, it's the seals that feed the people!"

"It must seem odd to you," replied George. "It's a different world in the city. I have been there so long, I have forgotten how to hunt. Can I take the boy with me when I go off to trap a seal tomorrow?"

"We will both go with you," replied Kudlah. "The first seal will be yours to take to the zoo. If we get others, we will keep them for our food." He looked out across the ice, then up to the sky. "But I don't think we will want to go tomorrow." Without explaining, he went inside the house.

"What's wrong with going after seals tomorrow?" George asked Kyo.

"It's the weather," the boy answered.

"But the sky is clear and the winds are dying. Tomorrow should be very warm and sunny."

"Yes, Uncle, that is what is wrong with it. The ice will be soupy. Traveling will be difficult."

"I see," said George. "I have forgotten

these things." He started hammering again.

Kyo worked with his uncle for the rest of the day. As the sun was setting they stood before the finished seal cage.

"Can I go inside?" the boy asked his uncle.

"Sure." George laughed. He unlatched the door and held it open for his nephew. Kyo crawled inside and asked George to close the door behind him. "But don't lock it!" he cried.

"I won't," George replied, and he went into the house to visit with his sister and brother-in-law.

Kyo sat in the cage and watched the sun dip behind the hills. The wind made a soft, high whine as it passed through the wire. Kyo leaned back and pressed his feet against the opposite side. He pushed with all his strength, but the wood and wire stayed firmly meshed. It was a strong cage, and he could see that he was no match for it. Could it hold a seal? he wondered. He crawled out and joined his parents and uncle in the house.

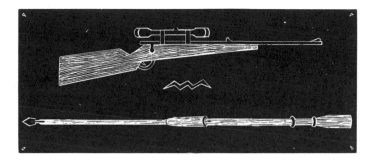

It was another two days before the
weather changed. Kyo heard his father speak
to George when the morning was still dark.
Soon George's big black boots were *thunk*ing
on the floor. The sharp noises approached
Kyo's bed and stopped. George's big hand
shook Kyo's shoulder.

"Wake up, Kyo, and we'll be seal hunting by daylight."

Kyo pulled his head under the warm
covers and pretended he was asleep. George
wasn't fooled.

"I know you're awake, Nephew. If the
seals are as hard to find as I'm told, we'd

better get going soon." He slid his arms under the boy, blankets and all, and lifted him up. George walked to the door and threw it open, letting in a blast of cold air. He carried Kyo outside.

"What are you hiding from?" asked George. "It's a beautiful day!"

Kyo pulled the covers back from his head and looked out. Stars shone brightly in the west, but faded in the pale gray southeastern sky. He giggled to be outside in his bedclothes. George held him firmly in his strong arms and began to swing him back and forth as if getting ready to throw him into the snow.

"One, two, three . . ."

"Wait!" yelled Kyo, laughing. "I'll get up!" So George took him back into the house.

An hour later Kudlah and George left the house on the snowmobile, pulling Kyo behind them on the sledge with the cage. Kyo's heart quickened as George steered toward the path to Tooky's hole, but Kudlah guided him in a different direction.

George had noticed Kyo's tracks leading to the hole.

"Those must be your small footprints," he yelled back to the boy, slowing the machine so he could be heard. "Where do they lead?"

"To a fishing place," answered Kyo. "But we don't want to go there."

"Is it a good fishing place?" asked George.

"Not a very good one," Kyo replied.

Their route took them around the base of a long mountain ridge. There they left the snowmobile and walked out on the ice. George carried a rifle and Kudlah carried a harpoon like Kyo's, only larger. Kyo wore a knapsack containing their lunch.

The settlement disappeared from view behind them. Kudlah told stories about the previous year's seal hunts. By the time they stopped at a seal breathing hole, Kyo was hungry.

"Here we are," said Kudlah. "This is a

good place to wait for seals." Kyo took a white cloth from inside the knapsack and unwrapped his lunch. George used a pick to widen the tiny hole. Kudlah went to look for others.

"I thought you wanted a *live* seal," Kyo asked, eyeing the gun suspiciously.

"I do. My gun shoots darts that will put the seal to sleep. The animal wakes up unharmed several hours later.

"When one comes and we shoot it, I'll hurry back to get the snowmobile and cage. We'll put the seal in the cage, so when it wakes up it can't get away."

George put down the pick and took a small box out of his pocket. Inside were plastic darts, each sporting a sharp needle.

"These will put the seal to sleep. See how small the needle is? The seal won't even feel it."

Kyo reached for one, but his uncle grabbed his hand. "Oh, no you don't." George laughed. "I don't want *you* to go to sleep!" He loaded the gun and put the box back in his pocket.

Kyo munched hungrily while George got chunks of snow for them to hide behind. Then they settled down away from the hole to wait. Kyo figured it would be a long wait, but he didn't tell his uncle that. He felt certain that the seals would not come.

They lay behind the snow blinds all that day and the next. Not one seal poked its nose up through the hole. As they set out for the third day, Kudlah told them he would be going inland to try to intercept caribou.

"You have heard enough hunting stories to remind you how to hunt," Kudlah told George.

Outwardly Kyo was calm, but inside he fretted. Had he made a mistake not to kill Tooky when he first saw her? Had he been wrong to tell the seal to stay away? He hoped that other game would cross his father's path.

At the same time, he missed his seal

friend. Would she come to visit him when his uncle left? What if he didn't leave for many weeks?

George and Kyo sped across the snow and ice on the snowmobile. The wind whipped at Kyo's face and blew his hood from his head. He automatically reached for the hood but stopped when he realized that his ears were not cold. The wind was getting warmer.

Kyo smiled and let the wind play with his ears and hair. With this warm wind and the sun staying longer in the sky, he thought happily, the ice would begin to break up. George couldn't stay too much longer, Kyo knew. Soon it would be dangerous to hunt for seals on the ice.

And once the ice was gone, he realized, seals would be much harder to catch. George would have to postpone his hunt until the ice settled in again in the fall. Maybe he'd change his mind or forget about capturing a seal by then.

George stopped the machine. "It's your turn to drive," he said to his nephew.

"Really? You want me to drive?" Kyo was astounded. His uncle got off the seat so Kyo could slide forward. George showed him how to start the snowmobile, increase and decrease the speed, and steer.

"Don't turn too sharply," he warned the boy, "or we might land in the snow with the machine on top of us. And if you start feeling scared, you'll know you're going too fast." George climbed on behind the boy, and they were off.

Kyo was thrilled as they flew over the snow, everything passing in a white blur. He tried zigzagging, drove up and down hills, and made a big circle, laughing hard all the way around. Then George tapped him on the shoulder and pointed toward their destination. Kyo steered the snowmobile toward it and drove as fast as he dared.

When he stopped the engine Kyo's ears were ringing. He shook his head to clear them. George chuckled. "You get used to that after you've ridden one of these for a while."

"It's fun," said Kyo, "but I don't think I'd ever get used to the noise."

"Which would you rather have, the speed of the snowmobile or the quiet of the dogsled?" George asked.

Kyo thought of the whisper of a sled pulled over the snow by panting dogs. "I like the quiet dogsled," he answered, and George laughed again.

"What's so funny?" Kyo felt hurt.

"I'm sorry, Kyo. Nothing's funny. You made a good choice, and I'm laughing at myself for preferring the noise. While I'm here, maybe you can take me for a ride on the dogsled. I haven't done that since I was a boy. But now let's get to our hunting place."

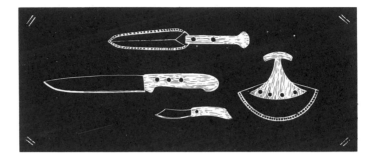

No seals appeared that day either. When Kyo got fidgety after lunch, he took out his knife and carving stone.

George heard Kyo's knife scratching.

"What are you doing?" he asked.

"Letting the seal out," murmured Kyo. George frowned at the boy hunched intently over his hands.

"Kyo, are you sure this is a good place for finding a seal?" asked George. "This is our third day here and we haven't seen so much as a whisker."

"This is a good place to be," asserted

Kyo, hoping his uncle wouldn't ask him any more questions about seal hunting.

"Well, tomorrow I think we should find someplace new," George said, pulling on his mustache. "In this spot we aren't having much luck."

Kyo couldn't fall asleep that night. When he heard deep snores from his uncle's bedroll on the floor across the room, Kyo slipped out of bed, went to the window, and parted the curtains.

The world outside was lit by an eerie silver glow. A big round disc of a moon hung in the sky. The snoring stopped, and Kyo heard rustling from George's bed. Turning, he saw the moonlight shining on his uncle's face.

Kyo quickly closed the curtains. The snoring resumed, and he put on his clothes as soundlessly as he could. Then he pulled on his boots and parka, eased the door open just enough for him to squeeze through, and found himself out in the nighttime glow.

He set out directly for Tooky's hole in the ice. Halfway there he remembered that if she had not been using the hole, it would have closed up, and he had not brought the pick. Still, he hurried on to their meeting place.

The hole was blocked by new ice, just as Kyo had expected. His throat tightened when he saw the frozen barrier. Sitting on the edge of the hole, he brought his heel down as hard as he could, but it bounced off the surface.

He leaned back, raising both feet high, and tried to smash the ice again. It didn't even crack. He considered jumping on the ice to break it open, but he knew that if he succeeded he'd likely drown.

"I'm not a seal," he said aloud. His words sounded small and lost in the strange night air. He lay on his belly and rubbed the surface of the ice with his mitten like he would wipe steam off his mother's mirror, hoping for a view of his friend below the surface.

"I don't know if you can hear me, Tooky," he said to the ice blocking his way, "but I'm doing my best to keep my uncle away from you. Keep checking this hole, Tooky, and when you see it open you'll know it's safe to come up and visit with me again. I don't know how long it will be, and I hope you don't give up. Please keep checking. I miss you!"

Kyo jumped up and started running back to his house. He stopped shortly, though, and ran back to the hole.

"I love you!" he called to his friend, and headed for the house again. As he ran the world darkened. He looked up to see the moon disappear behind a blanket of clouds. Snowflakes fell all around him. He slowed his pace as it got harder to see the path through the flurrying snow.

As Kyo reached his small dark house,

the air cleared and the brightness returned.
He turned to look out at the ice. Millions of
freshly fallen flakes sparkled in the moonlight. Suddenly very sleepy, Kyo slipped inside the warm house and got into bed.

*S*mack *smack! Thwack THWACK!*
Kyo opened his eyes hoping to see Tooky
clapping her flippers, but instead he saw his
mother making bread by the stove. He
quickly glanced over at his uncle's sleeping
place on the floor and sat up with a start
when he saw it was empty.

"Mama, where's my uncle?" Kyo asked
worriedly. Annawee answered without turning from her dough.

"He's off seal hunting. He tried to wake
you, but you slept as soundly as a baby. You

can follow him after you eat. He didn't take his snowmobile, and he left good tracks in the snow that fell last night."

Tracks! Kyo thought. *I* left tracks last night! He'll see them.

Kyo jumped out of bed and pulled on his clothes.

"Can I take my breakfast with me, Mama? I want to go help my uncle. I don't want to miss anything." He made his eyes as big as he could, but he didn't have to worry about convincing her.

"I'm glad you want to help him. It's rare that we get to see Ahko." She wrapped generous portions of breakfast in a clean towel, which Kyo stuffed into his parka.

"Goodbye!"

He ran out the door with his parka half open, pulling his mittens on his hands. He saw the tracks immediately: two sets of boots, big ones over little ones, following the path to Tooky's hole.

Kyo started to run down the path but changed his mind, going to the snowmobile instead. He jumped on the seat and sat for a moment, trying to remember how to start the engine. He turned the key, and the machine wheezed, coughed, and was silent. He tried again, and this time the whole thing shook and sputtered and growled—then was still. Kyo swung off the seat and kicked one of the runners.

"You have to start!" he shouted at the hulk of metal. Glancing at the house, Kyo saw Annawee's face appear briefly in the window. Before she reached the door Kyo was back on the snowmobile seat, turning the key. This time he remembered to turn the throttle.

The engine burst into its loud growl. Annawee's shouts were lost in the snowmobile roar as Kyo turned the throttle more and the machine lurched forward, pulling the sledge and cage away from the house and toward the great ice.

The world flew by. Thrilled by the speed, Kyo forgot for a moment that there was any danger, either to himself or to his friend at the end of the path. Rounding a protruding slab of ice, Kyo felt the machine lift slightly off one runner. Scared that he might tip over, he slowed down a little.

George came into view. He was thrusting a pick into Tooky's old breathing hole to reopen it. Stunned by George's action and feeling helpless to stop him, Kyo let the snowmobile slide to a halt.

George finished hacking at the ice and looked up. He waved to Kyo, stepped back from the reopened hole, and picked up his rifle. Kyo jumped down and ran toward George, hoping that Tooky would not appear.

Just then her round head popped up in the hole.

"Don't come up!" Kyo tried to yell, but the words caught in his throat. Tooky slid onto the ice and began her awkward lope toward the boy.

"No!" he cried, and she stopped, confused. George lifted his gun and the movement caught the seal's eye. She whirled and bobbed quickly toward the hole.

George fired, dropped the gun, and raced toward the seal, who continued toward her escape, slowing as she reached it. George dove onto the ice and grabbed her tail just as her head dipped into the water.

"Kyo!" he yelled. "Come and help me pull her out! She'll die if she falls in."

Kyo reached them just seconds later. Together he and his uncle heaved and pulled the heavy, limp animal safely onto the ice.

Kyo sank down beside the still form.

"Whew! That was close!" panted George. He too sat down beside the seal.

"She looks dead."

"Oh, no, Kyo. Remember, I told you that the darts only put the seal to sleep for a few hours. She hasn't been hurt at all."

Kyo wiped his eyes and nose on his sleeve. George glanced at the snowmobile and back to Kyo.

"You sure surprised me when you came flying down here on my machine. But then I could tell you were a smart boy. You learned quickly how to drive it."

Kyo was silent. He stared down at Tooky, wishing she would jump up and dive into the water before anyone could stop her.

"I'm not angry that you drove the snow-mobile out here, Kyo. That was quick thinking. I'm just glad you didn't get hurt. You knew I'd find a seal here, didn't you? Or is there another boy with boots your size who walks out here often, sometimes with only the moon to light his way?"

Kyo ignored his uncle, who stood up and went to retrieve the gun. Kyo put his ear against Tooky and listened for her heartbeat. It was strong and even. Then he put his ear to her nose and felt her warm breath.

Satisfied that the seal was alive, Kyo sat up, his thoughts racing. He was afraid to tell his uncle that Tooky was a friend. George would never believe him. He would laugh at him or, worse, tell his parents and they would all have a good laugh at him during supper that night.

"Animals have a hard life," George had told him the day before. "They have to fight and struggle to survive." Maybe Tooky would be better off in the zoo after all, Kyo thought. Maybe she'd like having fish handed to her every day. Maybe fish are hard to find on her own. He wished he could just ask her, but he knew that even awake she could not answer him.

George drove the snowmobile up close to the seal, parking the cage beside her. "Give me a hand with her—say, Kyo, how did you know this seal was a female?"

"I've seen her before," Kyo said quietly. "And I won't help you put her in your rotten cage!" Kyo turned and ran off, away from his uncle and the sleeping seal and the settlement.

Shaking his head, George gently maneuvered the heavy seal into the cage. Then he started the engine and drove carefully back to the house.

Kyo walked in a wide circle that took him far out on the ice, then inland to the base of the mountains. He found a sunny spot out of the wind and sat down, took out his knife and stone, and began to carve.

Near dusk he stood up, stretched his legs, and started to climb. Stopping partway up the slope to catch his breath, he turned and faced the valley below. He picked out his own house among the others, all dark against the graying terrain. The snowmobile was parked near the house and George's figure moved beside it.

A shadow passed over Kyo, and he looked up to see a great snowy owl glide over his head. The huge bird's outspread wings beat slowly and firmly against the evening air.

Suddenly it dropped to the snow, talons first, then quickly lifted off with a small, white ball of fur wriggling in its grasp. The owl had caught its prey. It would eat that night.

Kyo realized he was hungry, too. Hours ago he'd consumed the food his mother had packed for him. He started down the mountainside.

A loud clamor of barking dogs greeted Kyo as he approached his home. He saw Tooky lying still in the cage. He hung his fingers on the wire and leaned his face against it.

George came out of the house just as Kyo turned to go inside. He mumbled a greeting to his uncle and brushed by him.

Annawee sat in her favorite chair, a kerosene lamp glowing on either side of her, needle in hand, cloth heaped in her lap. Kudlah sat bent over a snowshoe frame, weaving narrow strips of leather, pulling them taut and securing them to the frame. They both looked up as Kyo came in and watched him slowly remove his parka.

"You look troubled, Kyo," said his father.

"I'm sad," he said, nodding. "And hungry."

Kudlah put down the snowshoe and went to the stove, where he ladled steaming soup into a bowl and set it on the table for the tired boy. He sat at the table with Kyo and watched him pour spoonfuls of soup into his mouth without pause. When the bowl was empty, Kyo asked for more. "Just half a bowl, please." Kudlah filled it and sat down again. When that was gone, too, Kyo pushed away the bowl and looked at his father.

"I saw a big white owl on the mountainside catch a mouse for its supper and I didn't feel sad. I was happy for the owl because it flew so smoothly and had no other way to get food." He stopped, but Kudlah just waited. Annawee had set down her needle. Her hands lay still in her lap.

"My uncle was happy to catch the seal today, but I'm not pleased for him at all. He says she'll be happier when someone gives her fish every day, but I wonder if she doesn't like to swim fast and catch her own?"

No one spoke, and no one laughed.

"I've never seen a seal swim under water, but they sure are clumsy on land. They're really made to swim, aren't they? I bet they're graceful in the sea, like this!" Kyo picked up his spoon and made it swoop through the air.

"*Whoosh . . . whoosh . . . whoosh!*"

The door opened and George walked in, head hanging. Kudlah filled another bowl with soup and set it on the table for his brother-in-law. "Come eat, George. You must be hungry. Are you ready for the long trip back to the city tomorrow?"

George washed his hands and sat down heavily beside Kyo. "I am ready," he replied. "But the seal is not. She should have awakened by now. Something went wrong. She is dead."

Kyo jumped up and ran outside without stopping to put on his parka. The others stayed seated.

His heart pounding, Kyo unfastened the door to the cage and crawled inside, moving carefully around his friend. He bent to feel her breath on his ear. Nothing. He listened for a heartbeat and heard it, a little sluggish but steady.

Then he tilted his head again for a breath. It seemed like forever before he felt a gentle tickle against his skin. He waited, stock still, until he felt it again.

Sighing with relief, Kyo leaned back, stroking Tooky's head.

"Why won't you wake up?" He spoke to her still form. "I don't know how to help you, but first I want to get you out of this cage."

Kyo crawled out and stalked into the house.

"She isn't dead," he announced to the waiting adults, who looked surprised.

"Kyo," George said gently, "I know you're upset about this. But she isn't breathing—"

"She is, too!" Kyo interrupted. "You just have to be patient. You don't understand seals! Sometimes they don't breathe when they sleep. But she *will* wake up!" His voice shook, a little unsure, but he rushed on. "You have to help me move her. She will feel better when she's near the water."

"You have seen this animal before, Kyo?" asked Kudlah.

Kyo nodded his head.

"And she lets you get so close that you can watch how she breathes?"

50

"Yes." Kyo spoke quietly.

Kudlah wrinkled his brow pensively, then stood up.

"If the seal is dead, George, she'll be of no use to us. Her meat will be spoiled by the drug in your darts, and we must throw her back in the bay.

"And if she is alive"—he looked at Kyo—"perhaps the boy can wake her up."

Kudlah put on his parka and boots and left the house.

Annawee put aside her sewing and also got ready to go outside. George sat with his elbows on the table, head in his hands.

"Ahko!" Annawee spoke sharply to her brother. "Let us do what Kudlah says." George got up slowly and followed the others outside.

In the light of the rising moon the seal did indeed look dead. "We're going to help you now, Tooky," Kyo whispered through the wire.

As George climbed on the snowmobile, Kyo said to his father, "I want to move her with the dog team."

"All right," agreed Kudlah.

With four of them working, the sledge was unharnessed from the snowmobile and hitched up to the dogs in no time. Kudlah handed the traces to his son.

"You know how to do this, Kyo. George, here is your chance for a dogsled ride."

Eagerly Kyo stepped up onto the sledge. George got on, too, and sat down. Commanding the restless dogs to run, Kyo guided the sledge away from the house. He let the dogs go as fast as they wanted, and he looked back often to check on the seal. When the hole was in sight, Kyo slowed the team and brought the sledge to a halt.

"I have to unhitch the dogs so Tooky won't be scared when she wakes up," Kyo said to his uncle. He jumped down and began to free the sledge.

"The seal—what do you call her, Tooky?—won't wake up, Kyo. I'm afraid that the sleeping medicine was too strong for her." Kyo either didn't hear his uncle or ignored him. He unhitched the dogs from the sledge but kept them harnessed together.

"Here," Kyo said, holding out the traces to his uncle. "I need your help. Take the dogs to the house. Please."

Reluctantly George did as the boy asked. He led the dogs away from the sledge but stopped when he'd gone about fifty yards.

Kyo climbed back into the cage. Cradling the seal's head in his lap, he sang a song his mother used to sing to him.

Wake up, sleepyhead,
Wake up, dreaming one.
The sky is shining now—
Come outside and see the sun!

Three times Kyo sang the verse. On the fourth, Tooky opened her eyes and picked up her head. Kyo nudged her gently toward the cage door. The seal wriggled her body backward through the opening.

Seeing the animal leave the cage, the dogs and George rushed forward to prevent her escape. Kyo looked up to see the yapping dogs approaching and commanded them to halt. The dogs obeyed, and George stopped behind them.

On the ice now, Tooky sniffed in different directions as if to get her bearings. Kyo scrambled out of the cage, clapped his mittens together, and laughed. Then he dashed ahead, and Tooky skittered along behind him. George started after them again, but this time he stopped himself and watched them go.

When they reached Tooky's hole in the ice, Kyo sat by the edge and faced the seal. She put her nose close to his and gently brushed it with her whiskers.

Leaning back, Kyo broke the thin layer of newly formed ice easily with the heel of his boot. He stood up and watched Tooky dive into the sea. Then he turned from the hole to follow his uncle, who was already walking back to the house, dog traces in hand, leaving the empty cage behind.

The snowmobile's deep growl woke Kyo the next morning. He jumped out of bed and ran to the window.

"He's not going yet, Kyo," said Anna-wee. "He's just fetching the cage. But he's leaving for the city right after breakfast."

While the family ate, Kyo watched his uncle through the steam rising from his hot-cakes. George joked with his brother-in-law and made plans to send fabric and new scissors to his sister while he ate the biggest stack of hotcakes Kyo had ever seen anybody eat. When George was done he turned to his nephew.

"I guess I won't be bringing a seal back to the city zoo after all, Kyo."

Kyo dropped his head, ashamed that he'd interfered with his uncle's dream, but relieved that the seal would remain in the sea.

"But I remember now what it was like to grow up here as a boy," he said, smiling at his sister.

"Thanks for showing me your special hunting spots," he said to Kudlah. To Kyo he said, "Thanks for giving me a ride on the dogsled I'll never forget." Kyo looked up at his uncle and relaxed when he saw the man's wide grin.

George stood up, hugged his sister and brother-in-law, and picked up Kyo.

"You don't have to leave without a seal," Kyo told him. He wriggled out of his uncle's arms, ran to his bed, and reached under his pillow for the finished stone seal carving.